Alfred Tennyson

The Cup

And, the falcon

Alfred Tennyson

The Cup
And, the falcon

ISBN/EAN: 9783337424206

Printed in Europe, USA, Canada, Australia, Japan

Cover: Foto ©Andreas Hilbeck / pixelio.de

More available books at **www.hansebooks.com**

THE CUP

AND

THE FALCON

BY

ALFRED
LORD TENNYSON

POET LAUREATE

London
MACMILLAN AND CO.
1884

THE CUP

A TRAGEDY

𝔈   B

"THE CUP" WAS PRODUCED AT THE LYCEUM THEATRE, UNDER THE MANAGEMENT OF MR. HENRY IRVING, JANUARY 3, 1881, WITH THE FOLLOWING CAST :—

GALATIANS.

SYNORIX, *an ex-Tetrarch* . . MR. HENRY IRVING.
SINNATUS, *a Tetrarch* . . . MR. TERRIS.
Attendant . . . . . MR. HARWOOD.
Boy . . . . . . MISS BROWN.
Maid . . . . . MISS HARWOOD.
PHŒBE . . . . . MISS PAUNCEFORT.
CAMMA, *wife of Sinnatus, afterwards Priestess in the Temple of Artemis* MISS ELLEN TERRY.

ROMANS.

ANTONIUS, *a Roman General* . MR. TYARS.
PUBLIUS . . . . . MR. HUDSON.
Nobleman . . . . . MR. MATHESON. ·
Messenger . . . . . MR. ARCHER.

ACT I.

SCENE I.—*Distant View of a City of Galatia.* (*Afternoon.*)
,, II.—*A Room in the Tetrarch's House.* (*Evening.*)
,, III.—*Same as Scene I.* (*Dawn.*)

ACT II.

SCENE—*Interior of the Temple of Artemis.*

THE CUP.

ACT I.

SCENE I.—*Distant View of a City of Galatia.*

As the curtain rises, Priestesses are heard singing in the
  Temple. Boy discovered on a pathway among Rocks,
  picking grapes. A party of Roman Soldiers, guarding
  a prisoner in chains, come down the pathway and exeunt.

Enter SYNORIX (*looking round*). *Singing ceases.*

SYNORIX.

Pine, beech and plane, oak, walnut, apricot,

Vine, cypress, poplar, myrtle, bowering-in

The city where she dwells. She past me here

Three years ago when I was flying from

My Tetrarchy to Rome.　I almost touch'd her—

A maiden slowly moving on to music

Among her maidens to this Temple—O Gods!

She is my fate—else wherefore has my fate

Brought me again to her own city?—married

Since—married Sinnatus, the Tetrarch here—

But if he be conspirator, Rome will chain,

Or slay him.　I may trust to gain her then

When I shall have my tetrarchy restored

By Rome, our mistress, grateful that I show'd her

The weakness and the dissonance of our clans,

And how to crush them easily.　Wretched race!

And once I wish'd to scourge them to the bones.

But in this narrow breathing-time of life

Is vengeance for its own sake worth the while,

If once our ends are gain'd? and now this cup—

I never felt such passion for a woman.

[Brings out a cup and scroll from under his cloak.

What have I written to her?

[Reading the scroll.

"To the admired Camma, wife of Sinnatus, the Tetrarch, one who years ago, himself an adorer of our great goddess, Artemis, beheld you afar off worshipping in her Temple, and loved you for it, sends you this cup rescued from the burning of one of her shrines in a city thro' which he past with the Roman army : it is the cup we use in our marriages. Receive it from one who cannot at present write himself other than

"A GALATIAN SERVING BY FORCE IN THE ROMAN LEGION."

[Turns and looks up to Boy.

Boy, dost thou know the house of Sinnatus?

BOY.

These grapes are for the house of Sinnatus—

Close to the Temple.

SYNORIX.

Yonder?

BOY.

Yes.

SYNORIX (*aside*).

That I

With all my range of women should yet shun

To meet her face to face at once!   My boy,

[*Boy comes down rocks to him.*

Take thou this letter and this cup to Camma,

The wife of Sinnatus.

BOY.

Going or gone to-day

To hunt with Sinnatus.

SYNORIX.

That matters not.

Take thou this cup and leave it at her doors.

[*Gives the cup and scroll to the Boy.*

BOY.

I will, my lord. [*Takes his basket of grapes and exit.*

Enter ANTONIUS.

ANTONIUS (*meeting the Boy as he goes out*).

Why, whither runs the boy?

Is that the cup you rescued from the fire?

SYNORIX.

I send it to the wife of Sinnatus,

One half besotted in religious rites.

You come here with your soldiers to enforce

The long-withholden tribute : you suspect

This Sinnatus of playing patriotism,

Which in your sense is treason.   You have yet

No proof against him : now this pious cup

Is passport to their house, and open arms

To him who gave it ; and once there I warrant

I worm thro' all their windings.

ANTONIUS.

If you prosper,

Our Senate, wearied of their tetrarchies,

Their quarrels with themselves, their spites at Rome,

Is like enough to cancel them, and throne

One king above them all, who shall be true

To the Roman : and from what I heard in Rome,

This tributary crown may fall to you.

SYNORIX.

The king, the crown ! their talk in Rome ? is it so?

[ANTONIUS *nods.*

Well—I shall serve Galatia taking it,

And save her from herself, and be to Rome

More faithful than a Roman.

> [*Turns and sees* CAMMA *coming.*
>
> Stand aside,

Stand aside; here she comes!

> [*Watching* CAMMA *as she enters*
> *with her Maid.*

CAMMA (*to Maid*).

Where is he, girl?

MAID.

You know the waterfall

That in the summer keeps the mountain side,

But after rain o'erleaps a jutting rock

And shoots three hundred feet.

CAMMA.

The stag is there?

MAID.

Seen in the thicket at the bottom there
But yester-even.

CAMMA.

Good then, we will climb
The mountain opposite and watch the chase.

[*They descend the rocks and exeunt.*

SYNORIX (*watching her*).

(*Aside.*) The bust of Juno and the brows and eyes
Of Venus; face and form unmatchable!

ANTONIUS.

Why do you look at her so lingeringly?

SYNORIX.

To see if years have changed her.

ANTONIUS (*sarcastically*).

Love her, do you?

SYNORIX.

I envied Sinnatus when he married her.

ANTONIUS.

She knows it ?   Ha !

SYNORIX.

She—no, nor ev'n my face.

ANTONIUS.

Nor Sinnatus either ?

SYNORIX.

No, nor Sinnatus.

ANTONIUS.

Hot-blooded !   I have heard them say in Rome,

That your own people cast you from their bounds,

For some unprincely violence to a woman,

As Rome did Tarquin.

SYNORIX.

Well, if this were so,

I here return like Tarquin—for a crown.

ANTONIUS.

And may be foil'd like Tarquin, if you follow

Not the dry light of Rome's straight-going policy,

But the fool-fire of love or lust, which well

May make you lose yourself, may even drown you

In the good regard of Rome.

SYNORIX.

Tut—fear mé not;

I ever had my victories among women.

I am most true to Rome.

ANTONIUS (*aside*).

I hate the man!

What filthy tools our Senate works with! Still

I must obey them. (*Aloud.*) Fare you well. [*Going.*

SYNORIX.

Farewell !

ANTONIUS (*stopping*).

A moment !   If you track this Sinnatus

In any treason, I give you here an order

[*Produces a paper.*

To seize upon him. Let me sign it. (*Signs it.*) There

" Antonius leader of the Roman Legion."

[*Hands the paper to* SYNORIX.   *Goes
up pathway and exit.*

SYNORIX.

Woman again !—but I am wiser now.

No rushing on the game—the net,—the net.

[*Shouts of* "Sinnatus ! Sinnatus !"   *Then horn.*

Looking off stage.]   He comes, a rough, bluff,

simple-looking fellow.

If we may judge the kernel by the husk,

Not one to keep a woman's fealty when

Assailed by Craft and Love.   I'll join with him :

I may reap something from him—come upon *her*

Again, perhaps, to-day—*her*.   Who are with him ?

I see no face that knows me.   Shall I risk it ?

I am a Roman now, they dare not touch me.

I will.

Enter SINNATUS, HUNTSMEN *and hounds.*

Fair Sir, a happy day to you !

You reck but little of the Roman here,

While you can take your pastime in the woods.

SINNATUS.

Ay, ay, why not ?   What would you with me, man?

SYNORIX.

I am a life-long lover of the chase,

And tho' a stranger fain would be allow'd

To join the hunt.

SINNATUS.

Your name?

SYNORIX.

Strato, my name.

SINNATUS.

No Roman name?

SYNORIX.

A Greek, my lord; you know

That we Galatians are both Greek and Gaul.

[*Shouts and horns in the distance.*

SINNATUS.

Hillo, the stag! (*To* SYNORIX.) What, you are

all unfurnish'd?

Give him a bow and arrows—follow—follow.

[*Exit, followed by Huntsmen.*

SYNORIX.

Slowly but surely—till I see my way.

It is the one step in the dark beyond

Our expectation, that amazes us.

[*Distant shouts and horns.*

Hillo! Hillo!

[*Exit* SYNORIX. *Shouts and horns.*

———

SCENE II.—*A Room in the Tetrarch's House.*

Frescoed figures on the walls. Evening. Moonlight outside. A couch with cushions on it. A small table with
flagon of wine, cups, plate of grapes, etc., also the cup
of Scene I. A chair with drapery on it.

CAMMA *enters, and opens curtains of window.*

CAMMA.

No Sinnatus yet—and there the rising moon.

[Takes up a cithern and sits on couch. Plays
and sings.

" Moon on the field and the foam,

Moon on the waste and the wold,

Moon bring him home, bring him home

Safe from the dark and the cold,

Home, sweet moon, bring him home,

Home with the flock to the fold—

Safe from the wolf "——

(*Listening.*) Is he coming? I thought I heard

A footstep. No not yet. They say that Rome

Sprang from a wolf. I fear my dear lord mixt

With some conspiracy against the wolf.

This mountain shepherd never dream'd of Rome.

(*Sings.*) " Safe from the wolf to the fold "——

And that great break of precipice that runs

Thro' all the wood, where twenty years ago

C

Huntsman, and hound, and deer were all neck-broken!
Nay, here he comes.

Enter Sinnatus *followed by* Synorix.

Sinnatus (*angrily*).

  I tell thee, my good fellow,
My arrow struck the stag.

Synorix.

    But was it so?
Nay, you were further off: besides the wind
Went with *my* arrow.

Sinnatus.

  I am sure *I* struck him.

Synorix.

And I am just as sure, my lord, *I* struck him.
(*Aside.*) And I may strike your game when you are
  gone.

CAMMA.

Come, come, we will not quarrel about the stag.

I have had a weary day in watching you.

Yours must have been a wearier.   Sit and eat,

And take a hunter's vengeance on the meats.

SINNATUS.

No, no—we have eaten—we are heated.   Wine !

CAMMA.

Who is our guest ?

SINNATUS.

Strato he calls himself.

[CAMMA *offers wine to* SYNORIX,
while SINNATUS *helps himself.*]

SINNATUS.

I pledge you, Strato.	[*Drinks.*

SYNORIX.

And I you, my lord.   [*Drinks.*

SINNATUS (*seeing the cup sent to* CAMMA).

What's here?

CAMMA.

A strange gift sent to me to-day.

A sacred cup saved from a blazing shrine

Of our great Goddess, in some city where

Antonius past.   I had believed that Rome

Made war upon the peoples not the Gods.

SYNORIX.

Most like the city rose against Antonius,

Whereon he fired it, and the sacred shrine

By chance was burnt along with it.

SINNATUS.

Had you then

No message with the cup?

CAMMA.

Why, yes, see here.   [*Gives him the scroll.*

SINNATUS (*reads*).

"To the admired Camma,—beheld you afar off—
loved you—sends you this cup—the cup we use in
our marriages—cannot at present write himself other
than

"A GALATIAN SERVING BY FORCE IN THE ROMAN LEGION."

Serving by force! Were there no boughs to hang on,
Rivers to drown in?   Serve by force?   No force
Could make me serve by force.

SYNORIX.

How then, my lord?
The Roman is encampt without your city—
The force of Rome a thousand-fold our own.

Must all Galatia hang or drown herself?

And you a Prince and Tetrarch in this province——

SINNATUS.

Province !

SYNORIX.

Well, well, they call it so in Rome.

SINNATUS (*angrily*).

Province !

SYNORIX.

A noble anger ! but Antonius

To-morrow will demand your tribute—you,

Can you make war ?   Have you alliances ?

Bithynia, Pontus, Paphlagonia ?

We have had our leagues of old with Eastern kings.

There is my hand—if such a league there be.

What will you do ?

SINNATUS.

Not set myself abroach

And run my mind out to a random guest

Who join'd me in the hunt.   You saw my hounds

True to the scent ; and we have two-legg'd dogs

Among us who can smell a true occasion,

And when to bark and how.

SYNORIX.

My good Lord Sinnatus,

I once was at the hunting of a lion.

Roused by the clamour of the chase he woke,

Came to the front of the wood—his monarch mane

Bristled about his quick ears—he stood there

Staring upon the hunter.   A score of dogs

Gnaw'd at his ankles : at the last he felt

The trouble of his feet, put forth one paw,

Slew four, and knew it not, and so remain'd

Staring upon the hunter : and this Rome

Will crush you if you wrestle with her ; then

Save for some slight report in her own Senate

Scarce know what she has done.

　　　　　(*Aside.*) Would I could move him,

Provoke him any way ! (*Aloud.*) The Lady Camma,

Wise I am sure as she is beautiful,

Will close with me that to submit at once

Is better than a wholly-hopeless war,

Our gallant citizens murder'd all in vain,

Son, husband, brother gash'd to death in vain,

And the small state more cruelly trampled on

Than had she never moved.

　　　　　CAMMA.

　　　　　　　　　Sir, I had once

A boy who died a babe ; but were he living

And grown to man and Sinnatus will'd it, I

Would set him in the front rank of the fight

With scarce a pang.   (*Rises.*)   Sir, if a state submit

At once, she may be blotted out at once

And swallow'd in the conqueror's chronicle.

Whereas in wars of freedom and defence

The glory and grief of battle won or lost

Solders a race together—yea—tho' they fail,

The names of those who fought and fell are like

A bank'd-up fire that flashes out again

From century to century, and at last

May lead them on to victory—I hope so—

Like phantoms of the Gods.

SINNATUS.
                              Well spoken, wife.

SYNORIX (*bowing*).

Madam, so well I yield.

SINNATUS.

I should not wonder
If Synorix, who has dwelt three years in Rome
And wrought his worst against his native land,
Returns with this Antonius.

SYNORIX.

What is Synorix?

SINNATUS.

Galatian, and not know? This Synorix
Was Tetrarch here, and tyrant also—did
Dishonour to our wives.

SYNORIX.

Perhaps you judge him
With feeble charity : being as you tell me
Tetrarch, there might be willing wives enough
To feel dishonour, honour.

CAMMA.

Do not say so.

I know of no such wives in all Galatia.

There may be courtesans for aught I know

Whose life is one dishonour.

Enter ATTENDANT.

ATTENDANT (*aside*).

My lord, the men !

SINNATUS (*aside*).

Our anti-Roman faction ?

ATTENDANT (*aside*).

Ay, my lord.

SYNORIX (*overhearing*).

(*Aside.*) I have enough—their anti-Roman faction.

SINNATUS (*aloud*).

Some friends of mind would speak with me without.

You, Strato, make good cheer till I return.   [*Exit.*

SYNORIX.

I have much to say, no time to say it in.

First, lady, know myself am that Galatian

Who sent the cup.

CAMMA.

I thank you from my heart.

SYNORIX.

Then that I serve with Rome to serve Galatia.

That is my secret : keep it, or you sell me

To torment and to death.   [*Coming closer.*

For your ear only—

I love you—for your love to the great Goddess.

The Romans sent me here a spy upon you,

To draw you and your husband to your doom.

I'd sooner die than do it.

[*Takes out paper given him by Antonius.*

This paper sign'd

Antonius—will you take it, read it ? there !

CAMMA.

(*Reads*) " You are to seize on Sinnatus,—if—— "

SYNORIX.

(*Snatches paper.*) No more.

What follows is for no wife's eyes.   O Camma,

Rome has a glimpse of this conspiracy ;

Rome never yet hath spar'd conspirator.

Horrible ! flaying, scourging, crucifying——

CAMMA.

I am tender enough.   Why do you practise on me ?

SYNORIX.

Why should I practise on you? How you wrong me!

I am sure of being every way malign'd.

And if you should betray me to your husband——

CAMMA.

Will *you* betray him by this order?

SYNORIX.
                                        See,

I tear it all to pieces, never dream'd

Of acting on it.   [*Tears the paper.*

CAMMA.

I owe you thanks for ever.

SYNORIX.

Hath Sinnatus never told you of this plot?

CAMMA.

What plot?

SYNORIX.

A child's sand-castle on the beach

For the next wave—all seen,—all calculated,

All known by Rome.   No chance for Sinnatus.

CAMMA.

Why, said you not as much to my brave Sinnatus?

SYNORIX.

Brave—ay—too brave, too over-confident,

Too like to ruin himself, and you, and me !

Who else, with this black thunderbolt of Rome

Above him, would have chased the stag to-day

In the full face of all the Roman camp?

A miracle that they let him home again,

Not caught, maim'd, blinded him.

[CAMMA *shudders.*

(*Aside.*) I have made her tremble.

(*Aloud.*) I know they mean to torture him to death.

I dare not tell him how I came to know it;

I durst not trust him with—my serving Rome

To serve Galatia: you heard him on the letter.

Not say as much? I all but said as much.

I am sure I told him that his plot was folly.

I say it to you—you are wiser—Rome knows all,

But you know not the savagery of Rome.

CAMMA.

O—have you power with Rome? use it for him!

SYNORIX.

Alas! I have no such power with Rome. All that

Lies with Antonius.

[*As if struck by a sudden thought. Comes over to her.*

               He will pass to-morrow

In the gray dawn before the Temple doors.

You have beauty,—O great beauty,—and Antonius,

So gracious toward women, never yet

Flung back a woman's prayer.　Plead to him,

I am sure you will prevail.

CAMMA.

　　　　　　Still—I should tell

My husband.

SYNORIX.

　　Will he let you plead for him

To a Roman?

CAMMA.

　　I fear not.

SYNORIX.

　　　　　Then do not tell him.

Or tell him, if you will, when you return,

When you have charm'd our general into mercy,

D

And all is safe again.   O dearest lady,

[*Murmurs of* "Synorix! Synorix!" *heard outside.*

Think,—torture,—death,—and come.

CAMMA.
I will, I will.

And I will not betray you.

SYNORIX (*aside*).

(*As* SINNATUS *enters.*) Stand apart.

Enter SINNATUS *and* ATTENDANT.

SINNATUS.

Thou art that Synorix! One whom thou hast wrong'd

Without there, knew thee with Antonius.

They howl for thee, to rend thee head from limb.

SYNORIX.

I am much malign'd.   I thought to serve Galatia.

SINNATUS.

Serve thyself first, villain ! They shall not harm

My guest within my house. There! (*points to door*)

    there ! this door

Opens upon the forest ! Out, begone !

Henceforth I am thy mortal enemy.

SYNORIX.

However I thank thee (*draws his sword*); thou hast

    saved my life.   [*Exit.*

SINNATUS. .

(*To Attendant.*) Return and tell them Synorix is

    not here.   [*Exit Attendant.*

What did that villain Synorix say to you ?

CAMMA.

Is *he—that—*Synorix ?

SINNATUS.

Wherefore should you doubt it?

One of the men there knew him.

CAMMA.
                                    Only one,

And he perhaps mistaken in the face.

SINNATUS.

Come, come, could he deny it?   What did he say?

CAMMA.

What *should* he say?

SINNATUS.
                        What *should* he say, my wife!

He should say this, that being Tetrarch once

His own true people cast him from their doors

Like a base coin.

CAMMA.

Not kindly to them?

SINNATUS.

Kindly?

O the most kindly Prince in all the world!

Would clap his honest citizens on the back,

Bandy their own rude jests with them, be curious

About the welfare of their babes, their wives,

O ay—their wives—their wives.   What should he

say?

He should say nothing to my wife if I

Were by to throttle him!   He steep'd himself

In all the lust of Rome.   How should *you* guess

What manner of beast it is?

CAMMA.

Yet he seem'd kindly,

And said he loathed the cruelties that Rome

Wrought on her vassals.

SINNATUS.

Did he, *honest* man ?

CAMMA.

And you, that seldom brook the stranger here,

Have let him hunt the stag with you to-day.

SINNATUS.

I warrant you now, he said *he* struck the stag.

CAMMA.

Why no, he never touch'd upon the stag.

SINNATUS.

Why so I said, *my* arrow.   Well, to sleep.

[*Goes to close door.*

CAMMA.

Nay, close not yet the door upon a night

That looks half day.

SINNATUS.

True ; and my friends may spy him

And slay him as he runs.

CAMMA.

He is gone already.

Oh look,—yon grove upon the mountain,—white

In the sweet moon as with a lovelier snow !

But what a blotch of blackness underneath !

Sinnatus, you remember—yea, you must,

That there three years ago—the vast vine-bowers

Ran to the summit of the trees, and dropt

Their streamers earthward, which a breeze of May

Took ever and anon, and open'd out

The purple zone of hill and heaven ; there

You told your love ; and like the swaying vines—

Yea,—with our eyes,—our hearts, our prophet hopes

Let in the happy distance, and that all

But cloudless heaven which we have found together

In our three married years !   You kiss'd me there

For the first time.   Sinnatus, kiss me now.

SINNATUS.

First kiss.   (*Kisses her.*)   There then.   You talk

    almost as if it

Might be the last.

CAMMA.

Will you not eat a little ?

SINNATUS.

No, no, we found a goat-herd's hut and shared

His fruits and milk.   Liar !   You will believe

Now that he never struck the stag—a brave one

Which you shall see to-morrow.

CAMMA.

I rise to-morrow

In the gray dawn, and take this holy cup

To lodge it in the shrine of Artemis.

SINNATUS.

Good!

CAMMA.

If I be not back in half an hour,

Come after me.

SINNATUS.

What! is there danger?

CAMMA.

Nay,

None that I know: 'tis but a step from here

To the Temple.

SINNATUS.

All my brain is full of sleep.

Wake me before you go, I'll after you—

After *me* now !   [*Closes door and exit.*

CAMMA (*drawing curtains*).

Your shadow.   Synorix—

His face was not malignant, and he said

That men malign'd him.   Shall I go ?   Shall I go ?

Death, torture—

" He never yet flung back a woman's prayer "—

I go, but I will have my dagger with me.   [*Exit.*

———

SCENE III.—*Same as Scene I.   Dawn.*

Music and Singing in the Temple.

Enter SYNORIX *watchfully, after him* PUBLIUS *and*

SOLDIERS.

SYNORIX.

Publius !

PUBLIUS.

Here !

SYNORIX.

Do you remember what

I told you ?

PUBLIUS.

When you cry " Rome, Rome," to seize

On whomsoever may be talking with you,

Or man, or woman, as traitors unto Rome.

SYNORIX.

Right.   Back again.   How many of you are there?

PUBLIUS.

Some half a score.   [*Exeunt Soldiers and Publius.*

SYNORIX.

                    I have my guard about me.

I need not fear the crowd that hunted me

Across the woods, last night.   I hardly gain'd

The camp at midnight.   Will she come to me

Now that she knows me Synorix ?   Not if Sinnatus

Has told her all the truth about me.   Well,

I cannot help the mould that I was cast in.

I fling all that upon my fate, my star.

I know that I am genial, I would be

Happy, and make all others happy so

They did not thwart me.   Nay, she will not come.

Yet if she be a true and loving wife

She may, perchance, to save this husband.   Ay!

See, see, my white bird stepping toward the snare.

Why now I count it all but miracle,

That this brave heart of mine should shake me so,

As helplessly as some unbearded boy's

When first he meets his maiden in a bower.

Enter CAMMA (*with cup*).

SYNORIX.

The lark first takes the sunlight on his wing,

But you, twin sister of the morning star,

Forelead the sun.

CAMMA.

Where is Antonius?

SYNORIX.

Not here as yet.   You are too early for him.

[*She crosses towards Temple.*

SYNORIX.

Nay, whither go you now?

CAMMA.

                    To lodge this cup

Within the holy shrine of Artemis,

And so return.

SYNORIX.

                    To find Antonius here.

[*She goes into the Temple, he looks after her.*

The loveliest life that ever drew the light

From heaven to brood upon her, and enrich

Earth with her shadow!   I trust she *will* return.

These Romans dare not violate the Temple.

No, I must lure my game into the camp.

A woman I could live and die for.   What!

Die for a woman, what new faith is this?

I am not mad, not sick, not old enough

To doat on one alone.   Yes, mad for her,

Camma the stately, Camma the great-hearted,

So mad, I fear some strange and evil chance

Coming upon me, for by the Gods I seem

Strange to myself.

Re-enter CAMMA.

CAMMA.

Where is Antonius?

SYNORIX.

Where?   As I said before, you are still too early.

CAMMA.

Too early to be here alone with thee;

For whether men malign thy name, or no,

It bears an evil savour among women.

Where is Antonius? (*Loud.*)

SYNORIX.

           Madam, as you know

The camp is half a league without the city;

If you will walk with me we needs must meet

Antonius coming, or at least shall find him

There in the camp.

CAMMA.

           No, not one step with thee.

Where is Antonius? (*Louder.*)

SYNORIX (*advancing towards her*).

           Then for your own sake,

Lady, I say it with all gentleness,

And for the sake of Sinnatus your husband,

I must compel you.

CAMMA (*drawing her dagger*).

           Stay!—too near is death.

SYNORIX (*disarming her*).

Is it not easy to disarm a woman?

Enter SINNATUS (*seizes him from behind
by the throat*).

SYNORIX (*throttled and scarce audible*).

Rome! Rome!

SINNATUS.

Adulterous dog!

SYNORIX (*stabbing him with* CAMMA'S *dagger*).

What! will you have it?

[CAMMA *utters a cry and runs
to* SINNATUS.

SINNATUS (*falls backward*).

I have it in my heart—to the Temple—fly—

For *my* sake—or they seize on thee.   Remember!

Away—farewell!   [*Dies.*

E

CAMMA (*runs up the steps into the Temple,*
looking back).

Farewell!

SYNORIX (*seeing her escape*).

The women of the Temple drag her in.

Publius! Publius! No,

Antonius would not suffer me to break

Into the sanctuary.   She hath escaped.

[*Looking down at* SINNATUS.

"Adulterous dog!" that red-faced rage at me!

Then with one quick short stab—eternal peace.

So end all passions.   Then what use in passions?

To warm the cold bounds of our dying life

And, lest we freeze in mortal apathy,

Employ us, heat us, quicken us, help us, keep us

From seeing all too near that urn, those ashes

Which all must be.   Well used, they serve us well.

I heard a saying in Egypt, that ambition

Is like the sea wave, which the more you drink,

The more you thirst—yea—drink too much, as men

Have done on rafts of wreck—it drives you mad.

I will be no such wreck, am no such gamester

As, having won the stake, would dare the chance

Of double, or losing all.   The Roman Senate,

For I have always play'd into their hands,

Means me the crown.   And Camma for my bride—

The people love her—if I win her love,

They too will cleave to me, as one with her.

There then I rest, Rome's tributary king.

    [*Looking down on* SINNATUS.

Why did I strike him ?—having proof enough

Against the man, I surely should have left

That stroke to Rome. He saved my life too. Did

    he?

It seem'd so.   I have play'd the sudden fool.

And that sets her against me—for the moment.

Camma—well, well, I never found the woman

I could not force or wheedle to my will.

She will be glad at last to wear my crown.

And I will make Galatia prosperous too,

And we will chirp among our vines, and smile

At bygone things till that (*pointing to* SINNATUS)

    eternal peace.

Rome!   Rome!

Enter PUBLIUS *and* SOLDIERS.

Twice I cried Rome.   Why came ye not before?

PUBLIUS

Why come we now?   Whom shall we seize upon?

SYNORIX (*pointing to the body of* SINNATUS).

The body of that dead traitor Sinnatus.

Bear him away.

Music and Singing in Temple.

END OF ACT I.

ACT II.

SCENE.—*Interior of the Temple of Artemis.*

Small gold gates on platform in front of the veil before the colossal statue of the Goddess, and in the centre of the Temple a tripod altar, on which is a lighted lamp. Lamps (lighted) suspended between each pillar. Tripods, vases, garlands of flowers, etc., about stage. Altar at back close to Goddess, with two cups. Solemn music. Priestesses decorating the Temple.

Enter a PRIESTESS.

PRIESTESS.

Phœbe, that man from Synorix, who has been

So oft to see the Priestess, waits once more

Before the Temple.

PHŒBE.

We will let her know.

[*Signs to one of the Priestesses, who goes out.*

Since Camma fled from Synorix to our Temple,

And for her beauty, stateliness, and power,

Was chosen Priestess here, have you not mark'd

Her eyes were ever on the marble floor?

To-day they are fixt and bright—they look straight

out.

Hath she made up her mind to marry him?

PRIESTESS.

To marry him who stabb'd her Sinnatus.

You will not easily make me credit that.

PHŒBE.

Ask her.

Enter CAMMA *as Priestess* (*in front of the curtains*).

PRIESTESS.

You will not marry Synorix?

CAMMA.

My girl, I am the bride of Death, and only

Marry the dead.

PRIESTESS.

Not Synorix then?

CAMMA.

My girl,

At times this oracle of great Artemis

Has no more power than other oracles

To speak directly.

PHŒBE.

Will you speak to him,

The messenger from Synorix who waits

Before the Temple?

CAMMA.

Why not ?   Let him enter.

[*Comes forward on to step by tripod.*

Enter a MESSENGER.

MESSENGER (*kneels*).

Greeting and health from Synorix!   More than once
You have refused his hand.   When last I saw you,
You all but yielded.   He entreats you now
For your last answer.   When he struck at Sinnatus—
As I have many a time declared to you—
He knew not at the moment who had fasten'd
About his throat—he begs you to forget it
As scarce his act :—a random stroke : all else
Was love for you : he prays you to believe him.

CAMMA.

I pray him to believe—that I believe him.

MESSENGER.

Why that is well.   You mean to marry him?

CAMMA.

I mean to marry him—if that be well.

MESSENGER.

This very day the Romans crown him king

For all his faithful services to Rome.

He wills you then this day to marry him,

And so be throned together in the sight

Of all the people, that the world may know

You twain are reconciled, and no more feuds

Disturb our peaceful vassalage to Rome.

CAMMA.

To-day?   Too sudden.   I will brood upon it.

When do they crown him?

MESSENGER.

Even now.

CAMMA.

And where?

MESSENGER.

Here by your temple.

CAMMA.

Come once more to me

Before the crowning,—I will.answer you.

[*Exit Messenger.*

PHŒBE.

Great Artemis! O Camma, can it be well,

Or good, or wise, that you should clasp a hand

Red with the sacred blood of Sinnatus?

CAMMA.

Good! mine own dagger driven by Synorix found

All good in the true heart of Sinnatus,

And quench'd it there for ever.   Wise !

Life yields to death and wisdom bows to Fate,

Is wisest, doing so.   Did not this man

Speak well?   We cannot fight imperial Rome,

But he and I are both Galatian-born,

And tributary sovereigns, he and I

Might teach this Rome—from knowledge of our

    people—

Where to lay on her tribute—heavily here

And lightly there.   Might I not live for that,

And drown all poor self-passion in the sense

Of public good?

PHŒBE.

        I am sure you will not marry him.

CAMMA.

Are you so sure ?   I pray you wait and see.

[*Shouts* (*from the distance*), "Synorix! Synorix!"

CAMMA.

Synorix, Synorix! So they cried Sinnatus

Not so long since—they sicken me. The One

Who shifts his policy suffers something, must

Accuse himself, excuse himself; the Many

Will feel no shame to give themselves the lie.

PHŒBE.

Most like it was the Roman soldier shouted.

CAMMA.

Their shield-borne patriot of the morning star

Hang'd at mid-day, their traitor of the dawn

The clamour'd darling of their afternoon!

And that same head they would have play'd at ball

    with,

And kick'd it featureless—they now would crown.

[*Flourish of trumpets.*

Enter a Galatian NOBLEMAN *with crown on a cushion.*

NOBLE (*kneels*).

Greeting and health from Synorix.   He sends you

This diadem of the first Galatian Queen,

That you may feed your fancy on the glory of it,

And join your life this day with his, and wear it

Beside him on his throne.   He waits your answer.

CAMMA.

Tell him there is one shadow among the shadows,

One ghost of all the ghosts—as yet so new,

So strange among them—such an alien there,

So much of husband in it still—that if

The shout of Synorix and Camma sitting

Upon one throne, should reach it, *it* would rise

HE! . . . HE, with that red star between the ribs,

And my knife there—and blast the king and me,

And blanch the crowd with horror.   I dare not, sir!

Throne him——and then the marriage—ay and tell
   him

That I accept the diadem of Galatia—

[All are amazed.

Yea, that ye saw me crown myself withal.

[Puts on the crown.

I wait him his crown'd queen.

NOBLE.

So will I tell him.

[Exit.

Music.   Two Priestesses go up the steps before the shrine,
   draw the curtains on either side (discovering the Goddess),
   then open the gates and remain on steps, one on either
   side, and kneel.   A Priestess goes off and returns with
   a veil of marriage, then assists Phœbe to veil Camma.
   At the same time Priestesses enter and stand on either

side of the Temple.   Camma and all the Priestesses
kneel, raise their hands to the Goddess, and bow down.

[*Shouts,* " Synorix ! Synorix ! "   *All rise.*

CAMMA.

Fling wide the doors, and let the new-made children

Of our imperial mother see the show.

[*Sunlight pours through the doors.*

I have no heart to do it.   (*To Phœbe*).   Look for me!

[*Crouches.*   PHŒBE *looks out.*

[*Shouts,* " Synorix ! Synorix ! "

PHŒBE.

He climbs the throne.   Hot blood, ambition, pride

So bloat and redden his face—O would it were

His third last apoplexy !.   O bestial !

O how unlike our goodly Sinnatus.

CAMMA (*on the ground*).

You wrong him surely ; far as the face goes

A goodlier-looking man than Sinnatus.

PHŒBE (*aside*).

How dare she say it ?   I could hate her for it

But that she is distracted.   [*A flourish of trumpets.*

CAMMA.

Is he crown'd ?

PHŒBE.

Ay, there they crown him.

[*Crowd without shout,* " Synorix ! Synorix ! "

CAMMA (*rises*).

[*A Priestess brings a box of spices to* CAMMA,
who throws them on the altar flame.

Rouse the dead altar-flame, fling in the spices,

Nard, Cinnamon, amomum, benzoin.

Let all the air reel into a mist of odour,

F

As in the midmost heart of Paradise.

Lay down the Lydian carpets for the king.

The king should pace on purple to his bride,

And music there to greet my lord the king. [*Music.*

(*To Phœbe.*) Dost thou remember when I wedded

    Sinnatus?

Ay, thou wast there—whether from maiden fears

Or reverential love for him I loved,

Or some strange second-sight, the marriage-cup

Wherefrom we make libation to the Goddess

So shook within my hand, that the red wine

Ran down the marble and lookt like blood, like blood.

PHŒBE.

I do remember your first-marriage fears.

CAMMA.

I have no fears at this my second marriage.

See here—I stretch my hand out—hold it there.

How steady it is!

PHŒBE.

Steady enough to stab him!

CAMMA.

O hush! O peace! This violence ill becomes

The silence of our Temple. Gentleness,

Low words best chime with this solemnity.

Enter a procession of Priestesses and Children bear-
ing garlands and golden goblets, and strewing
flowers.

Enter SYNORIX (*as King, with gold laurel-wreath*
crown and purple robes), *followed by* ANTONIUS,
PUBLIUS, *Noblemen, Guards, and the Popu-*
lace.

CAMMA.

Hail, King!

SYNORIX.

Hail, Queen!

The wheel of Fate has roll'd me to the top.

I would that happiness were gold, that I

Might cast my largess of it to the crowd!

I would that every man made feast to-day

Beneath the shadow of our pines and planes!

For all my truer life begins to-day.

The past is like a travell'd land now sunk

Below the horizon—like a barren shore

That grew salt weeds, but now all drown'd in love

And glittering at full tide—the bounteous bays

And havens filling with a blissful sea.

Nor speak I now too mightily, being King

And happy! happiest, Lady, in my power

To make you happy.

CAMMA.

Yes, sir.

SYNORIX.

Our Antonius,

Our faithful friend of Rome, tho' Rome may set

A free foot where she will, yet of his courtesy

Entreats he may be present at our marriage.

CAMMA.

Let him come—a legion with him, if he will.

(*To* ANTONIUS.) Welcome, my lord Antonius, to

   our Temple.

(*To* SYNORIX.) You on this side the altar. (*To*

   ANTONIUS.) You on that.

Call first upon the Goddess, Synorix.

[*All face the Goddess. Priestesses, Children, Populace,*
   and Guards kneel—the others remain standing.

SYNORIX.

O Thou, that dost inspire the germ with life,

The child, a thread within the house of birth,

And give him limbs, then air, and send him forth

The glory of his father—Thou whose breath

Is balmy wind to robe our hills with grass,

And kindle all our vales with myrtle-blossom,

And roll the golden oceans of our grain,

And sway the long grape-bunches of our vines,

And fill all hearts with fatness and the lust

Of plenty—make me happy in my marriage !

CHORUS (*chanting*).

Artemis, Artemis, hear him, Ionian Artemis !

CAMMA.

O Thou that slayest the babe within the womb

Or in the being born, or after slayest him

As boy or man, great Goddess, whose storm-voice

Unsockets the strong oak, and rears his root

Beyond his head, and strows our fruits, and lays

Our golden grain, and runs to sea and makes it

Foam over all the fleeted wealth of kings

And peoples, hear.

Whose arrow is the plague—whose quick flash
  splits

The mid-sea mast, and rifts the tower to the rock,

And hurls the victor's column down with him

That crowns it, hear.

Who causest the safe earth to shudder and gape,

And gulf and flatten in her closing chasm

Domed cities, hear.

Whose lava-torrents blast and blacken a province

To a cinder, hear.

Whose winter-cataracts find a realm and leave it

A waste of rock and ruin, hear.   I call thee

To make my marriage prosper to my wish !

CHORUS.

Artemis, Artemis, hear her, Ephesian Artemis !

CAMMA.

Artemis, Artemis, hear me, Galatian Artemis !

I call on our own Goddess in our own Temple.

CHORUS.

Artemis, Artemis, hear her, Galatian Artemis !

[*Thunder.   All rise.*

SYNORIX (*aside*).

Thunder !   Ay, ay, the storm was drawing hither

Across the hills when I was being crown'd.

I wonder if I look as pale as she ?

CAMMA

Art thou—still bent—on marrying ?

SYNORIX.

Surely—yet

These are strange words to speak to Artemis.

CAMMA.

Words are not always what they seem, my King.

I will be faithful to thee till thou die.

SYNORIX.

I thank thee, Camma,—I thank thee.

CAMMA (*turning to* ANTONIUS).

Antonius,

Much graced are we that our Queen Rome in you

Deigns to look in upon our barbarisms.

[*Turns, goes up steps to altar before the Goddess.*
Takes a cup from off the altar. Holds it to-
wards ANTONIUS. ANTONIUS *goes up to the*
foot of the steps, opposite to SYNORIX.

You see this cup, my lord.   [*Gives it to him.*

ANTONIUS.

Most curious !

The many-breasted mother Artemis

Emboss'd upon it.

CAMMA.

It is old, I know not

How many hundred years.   Give it me again.

It is the cup belonging our own Temple.

> [*Puts it back on altar, and takes up the cup*
> *of Act I.   Showing it to* ANTONIUS.

Here is another sacred to the Goddess,

The gift of Synorix; and the Goddess, being

For this most grateful, wills, thro' me her Priestess,

In honour of his gift and of our marriage,

That Synorix should drink from his own cup.

SYNORIX.

I thank thee, Camma,—I thank thee.

Camma.

For—my lord—

It is our ancient custom in Galatia

That ere two souls be knit for life and death,

They two should drink together from one cup,

In symbol of their married unity,

Making libation to the Goddess.   Bring me

The costly wines we use in marriages.

> [*They bring in a large jar of wine.*
> Camma *pours wine into cup.*

(*To* Synorix.) See here, I fill it.   (*To* Antonius.)

Will you drink, my lord?

Antonius.

I? Why should I? I am not to be married.

Camma.

But that might bring a Roman blessing on us.

ANTONIUS (*refusing cup*).

Thy pardon, Priestess !

CAMMA.

            Thou art in the right.

This blessing is for Synorix and for me.

See first I make libation to the Goddess,

                [*Makes libation.*

And now I drink.   [*Drinks and fills the cup again.*

            Thy turn, Galatian King.

Drink and drink deep—our marriage will be fruitful.

Drink and drink deep, and thou wilt make me happy.

      [SYNORIX *goes up to her.   She hands him*
          the cup.   He drinks.

SYNORIX.

There, Camma !   I have almost drain'd the cup—

A few drops left.

CAMMA.

Libation to the Goddess.

[*He throws the remaining drops on the
altar and gives* CAMMA *the cup.*

CAMMA (*placing the cup on the altar*).
Why then the Goddess hears.

[*Comes down and forward to tripod.*
ANTONIUS *follows.*

Antonius,

Where wast thou on that morning when I came

To plead to thee for Sinnatus's life,

Beside this temple half a year ago?

ANTONIUS.

I never heard of this request of thine.

SYNORIX (*coming forward hastily to foot of
tripod steps*).

I sought him and I could not find him.   Pray you,

Go on with the marriage rites.

CAMMA.

Antonius——

"Camma!" who spake?

ANTONIUS.

Not I.

PHŒBE.

Nor any here.

CAMMA.

I am all but sure that some one spake.   Antonius,

If you had found him plotting against Rome,

Would you have tortured Sinnatus to death?

ANTONIUS.

No thought was mine of torture or of death,

But had I found him plotting, I had counsell'd him

To rest from vain resistance.   Rome is fated

To rule the world.   Then, if he had not listen'd,

I might have sent him prisoner to Rome.

SYNORIX.

Why do you palter with the ceremony?

Go on with the marriage rites.

CAMMA.

      They are finish'd.

SYNORIX.

        How!

CAMMA.

Thou hast drunk deep enough to make me happy.

Dost thou not feel the love I bear to thee

Glow thro' thy veins?

SYNORIX.

The love I bear to thee

Glows thro' my veins since first I look'd on thee.

But wherefore slur the perfect ceremony?

The sovereign of Galatia weds his Queen.

Let all be done to the fullest in the sight

Of all the Gods. (*Starts.*)   This pain—what is it?—

again?

I had a touch of this last year—in—Rome.

Yes, yes. (*To* ANTONIUS.) Your arm—a moment—

It will pass.

I reel beneath the weight of utter joy—

This all too happy day, crown—queen at once.

[*Staggers.*

O all ye Gods—Jupiter!—Jupiter! [*Falls backward.*

CAMMA.

Dost thou cry out upon the Gods of Rome.

Thou art Galatian-born? Our Artemis

Has vanquish'd their Diana.

SYNORIX (*on the ground*).

I am poison'd.

She—close the Temple doors.   Let her not fly.

CAMMA (*leaning on tripod*).

Have I not drunk of the same cup with thee?

SYNORIX.

Ay, by the Gods of Rome and all the world,

She too—she too—the bride! the Queen! and I—

Monstrous!   I that loved her.

CAMMA.

I loved *him.*

SYNORIX.

O murderous mad-woman!   I pray you lift me

G

And make me walk awhile. I have heard these
   poisons

May be walk'd down.

        [ANTONIUS *and* PUBLIUS *raise him up.*

              My feet are tons of lead,

They will break in the earth—I am sinking—hold
   me—

Let me alone.

       [*They leave him ; he sinks down on ground.*

           Too late—thought myself wise—

A woman's dupe.   Antonius, tell the Senate

I have been most true to Rome—would have been
   true

To *her*—if—if——   [*Falls as if dead.*

    CAMMA (*coming and leaning over him*).

        So falls the throne of an hour.

SYNORIX (*half rising*).

Throne? is it thou? the Fates are throned, not

we—

Not guilty of ourselves—thy doom and mine—

Thou—coming my way too—Camma—good-night.

[*Dies.*

CAMMA (*upheld by weeping Priestesses*).

Thy way? poor worm, crawl down thine own black

hole

To the lowest Hell.   Antonius, is *he* there?

I meant thee to have follow'd—better thus.

Nay, if my people must be thralls of Rome,

He is gentle, tho' a Roman.

[*Sinks back into the arms of the Priestesses.*

ANTONIUS.

Thou art one

With thine own people, and tho' a Roman I

Forgive thee, Camma.

              CAMMA (*raising herself*).

                "CAMMA!"—why there again

I am most sure that some one call'd.   O women,

Ye will have Roman masters.   I am glad

I shall not see it.   Did not some old Greek

Say death was the chief good? He had my fate for it,

Poison'd.   (*Sinks back again*).   Have I the crown

        on?   I will go

To meet him, crown'd! crown'd victor of my will—

On my last voyage—but the wind has fail'd—

Growing dark too—but light enough to row.

Row to the blessed Isles! the blessed Isles!—

Sinnatus!

Why comes he not to meet me?   It is the crown

Offends him—and my hands are too sleepy

To lift it off.   [PHŒBE *takes the crown off.*

                    Who touch'd me then? I thank you.

                    [*Rises, with outspread arms.*

There—league on league of ever-shining shore

Beneath an ever-rising sun—I see him—

"Camma, Camma!" Sinnatus, Sinnatus!   [*Dies.*

THE END.

THE FALCON

"THE FALCON" WAS PRODUCED AT THE ST. JAMES'S
THEATRE, UNDER THE MANAGEMENT OF MESSRS.
HARE AND KENDAL, IN DECEMBER 1879, WITH THE
FOLLOWING CAST :—

THE COUNT FEDERIGO DEGLI
   ALBERIGHI   .   .   . MR. KENDAL.
FILIPPO, *Count's foster-brother* . MR. DENNY.
THE LADY GIOVANNA .   . MRS. KENDAL.
ELISABETTA, *the Count's nurse* MRS. GASTON MURRAY.

THE FALCON.

SCENE.—*An Italian Cottage. Castle and Mountains seen through Window.*

ELISABETTA discovered seated on stool in window darning. The COUNT with Falcon on his hand comes down through the door at back. A withered wreath on the wall.

ELISABETTA.

So, my lord, the Lady Giovanna, who hath been away so long, came back last night with her son to the castle.

COUNT.

Hear that, my bird ! Art thou not jealous of her ?

My princess of the cloud, my plumed purveyor,

My far-eyed queen of the winds—thou that canst

   soar

Beyond the morning lark, and howsoe'er

Thy quarry wind and wheel, swoop down upon him

Eagle-like, lightning-like—strike, make his feathers

Glance in mid heaven.   [*Crosses to chair.*

                 I would thou hadst a mate!

Thy breed will die with thee, and mine with me :

I am as lone and loveless as thyself. [*Sits in chair.*

Giovanna here ! Ay, ruffle thyself—*be* jealous !

Thou should'st be jealous of her. Tho' I bred thee

The full-train'd marvel of all falconry,

And love thee and thou me, yet if Giovanna

Be here again—No, no ! Buss me, my bird !

The stately widow has no heart for me.

Thou art the last friend left me upon earth—

No, nó again to that.   [*Rises and turns.*

My good old nurse,

I had forgotten thou wast sitting there.

ELISABETTA.

Ay, and forgotten thy foster-brother too.

COUNT.

Bird-babble for my falcon !   Let it pass.

What art thou doing there?

ELISABETTA.

Darning, your lordship.

We cannot flaunt it in new feathers now :

Nay, if we *will* buy diamond necklaces

To please our lady, we must darn, my lord.

This old thing here (*points to necklace round her neck*),

they are but blue beads—my Piero,

God rest his honest soul, he bought 'em for me,

Ay, but he knew I meant to marry him.

How couldst thou do it, my son ?   How couldst thou

do it ?

COUNT.

She saw it at a dance, upon a neck

Less lovely than her own, and long'd for it.

ELISABETTA.

She told thee as much ?

COUNT.

No, no—a friend of hers.

ELISABETTA.

Shame on her that she took it at thy hands,

She rich enough to have bought it for herself !

COUNT.

She would have robb'd me then of a great pleasure.

ELISABETTA.

But hath she yet return'd thy love?

COUNT.

Not yet!

ELISABETTA.

She should return thy necklace then.

COUNT.

Ay, if

She knew the giver; but I bound the seller

To silence, and I left it privily

At Florence, in her palace.

ELISABETTA.

And sold thine own

To buy it for her. She not know? She knows

There's none such other——

COUNT.

Madman anywhere.

Speak freely, tho' to call a madman mad

Will hardly help to make him sane again.

Enter FILIPPO.

FILIPPO.

Ah, the women, the women! Ah, Monna Giovanna,

you here again! you that have the face of an

angel and the heart of a—that's too positive! You

that have a score of lovers and have not a heart

for any of them—that's positive-negative: you that

have *not* the head of a toad, and *not* a heart like

the jewel in it—that's too negative; you that have

a cheek like a peach and a heart like the stone in

it—that's positive again—that's better!

ELISABETTA.

Sh—sh—Filippo!

FILIPPO (*turns half round*).

Here has our master been a-glorifying and a-velveting and a-silking himself, and a-peacocking and a-spreading to catch her eye for a dozen year, till he hasn't an eye left in his own tail to flourish among the peahens, and all along o' you, Monna Giovanna, all along o' you!

ELISABETTA.

Sh—sh—Filippo! Can't you hear that you are saying behind his back what you see you are saying afore his face?

COUNT.

Let him—he never spares me to my face!

FILIPPO.

No, my lord, I never spare your lordship to your lordship's face, nor behind your lordship's back, nor to right, nor to left, nor to round about and back to your lordship's face again, for I'm honest, your lordship.

COUNT.

Come, come, Filippo, what is there in the larder?

[ELISABETTA *crosses to fireplace and puts on wood.*

FILIPPO.

Shelves and hooks, shelves and hooks, and when I see the shelves I am like to hang myself on the hooks.

COUNT.

No bread?

FILIPPO.

Half a breakfast for a rat!

COUNT.

Milk?

FILIPPO.

Three laps for a cat !

COUNT.

Cheese ?

FILIPPO.

A supper for twelve mites.

COUNT.

Eggs ?

FILIPPO.

One, but addled.

COUNT.

No bird ?

FILIPPO.

Half a tit and a hern's bill.

COUNT.

Let be thy jokes and thy jerks, man ! Anything
or nothing ?

H

Filippo.

Well, my lord, if all-but-nothing be anything,
and one plate of dried prunes be all-but-nothing,
then there is anything in your lordship's larder at
your lordship's service, if your lordship care to call
for it.

Count.

Good mother, happy was the prodigal son,
For he return'd to the rich father ; I
But add my poverty to thine.   And all
Thro' following of my fancy.   Pray thee make
Thy slender meal out of those scraps and shreds
Filippo spoke of.   As for him and me,
There sprouts a salad in the garden still.
(*To the Falcon.*) Why didst thou miss thy quarry
    · yester-even ?

To-day, my beauty, thou must dash us down

Our dinner from the skies. Away, Filippo !

[*Exit, followed by* FILIPPO.

ELISABETTA.

I knew it would come to this. She has beggared

him. I always knew it would come to this! (*Goes*

up to table as if to resume darning, and looks out of

window.) Why, as I live, there is Monna Giovanna

coming down the hill from the castle. Stops and

stares at our cottage. Ay, ay ! stare at it : it's all

you have left us. Shame upon you ! *She* beauti-

ful ! sleek as a miller's mouse ! Meal enough,

meat enough, well fed ; but beautiful—bah ! Nay,

see, why she turns down the path through our little

vineyard, and I sneezed three times this morning.

Coming to visit my lord, for the first time in her

life too ! Why, bless the saints ! I'll be bound to confess her love to him at last. I forgive her, I forgive her ! I knew it would come to this—I always knew it must come to this ! (*Going up to door during latter part of speech and opens it.*) Come in, Madonna, come in. (*Retires to front of table and curtseys as the* LADY GIOVANNA *enters, then moves chair towards the hearth.*) Nay, let me place this chair for your ladyship.

[LADY GIOVANNA *moves slowly down stage, then crosses to chair, looking about her, bows as she sees the Madonna over fireplace, then sits in chair.*

LADY GIOVANNA.

Can I speak with the Count ?

ELISABETTA.

Ay, my lady, but won't you speak with the old woman first, and tell her all about it and make her happy? for I've been on my knees every day for these half-dozen years in hope that the saints would send us this blessed morning; and he always took you so kindly, he always took the world so kindly. When he was a little one, and I put the bitters on my breast to wean him, he made a wry mouth at it, but he took it so kindly, and your ladyship has given him bitters enough in this world, and he never made a wry mouth at you, he always took you so kindly—which is more than I did, my lady, more than I did—and he so handsome—and bless your sweet face, you look as beautiful this morning as the very Madonna her own self—and better late than never—but come when they will—then or now—it's all for the best, come when they will— they are made by the blessed saints—these mar- riages. *[Raises her hands.*

LADY GIOVANNA.

Marriages ?   I shall never marry again !

ELISABETTA (*rises and turns*).

Shame on her then !

LADY GIOVANNA.

Where is the Count ?

ELISABETTA.

Just gone

To fly his falcon.

LADY GIOVANNA.

Call him back and say

I come to breakfast with him.

ELISABETTA.

Holy mother !

To breakfast !   Oh sweet saints ! one plate of prunes !

Well, Madam, I will give your message to him.

[*Exit.*

LADY GIOVANNA.

His falcon, and I come to ask for his falcon,

The pleasure of his eyes—boast of his hand—

Pride of his heart—the solace of his hours—

His one companion here—nay, I have heard

That, thro' his late magnificence of living

And this last costly gift to mine own self,

[*Shows diamond necklace.*

He hath become so beggar'd, that his falcon

Ev'n wins his dinner for him in the field.

That must be talk, not truth, but truth or talk,

How can I ask for his falcon?

[*Rises and moves as she speaks.*

O my sick boy!

My daily fading Florio, it is thou

Hath set me this hard task, for when I say

What can I do—what can I get for thee?

He answers, "Get the Count to give me his
>   falcon,

And that will make me well."   Yet if I ask,

He loves me, and he knows I know he loves me !

Will he not pray me to return his love—

To marry him ?—(*pause*)—I can never marry him.

His grandsire struck my grandsire in a brawl

At Florence, and my grandsire stabb'd him there.

The feud between our houses is the bar

I cannot cross ; I dare not brave my brother,

Break with my kin.   My brother hates him,
>   scorns

The noblest-natured man alive, and I—

Who have that reverence for him that I scarce

Dare beg him to receive his diamonds back—

How can I, dare I, ask him for his falcon ?

>   [*Puts diamonds in her casket.*

Re-enter COUNT *and* FILIPPO. COUNT *turns to* FILIPPO.

COUNT.

Do what I said ; I cannot do it myself.

FILIPPO.

Why then, my lord, we are pauper'd out and out.

COUNT.

Do what I said !   [*Advances and bows low.*

Welcome to this poor cottage, my dear lady.

LADY GIOVANNA.

And welcome turns a cottage to a palace.

COUNT.

'Tis long since we have met !

LADY GIOVANNA.

                                 To make amends

I come this day to break my fast with you.

COUNT.

I am much honour'd—yes—   [*Turns to* FILIPPO.

Do what I told thee.   Must I do it myself?

FILIPPO.

I will, I will.   (*Sighs.*)   Poor fellow!   [*Exit.*

COUNT.

Lady, you bring your light into my cottage

Who never deign'd to shine into my palace.

My palace wanting you was but a cottage;

My cottage, while you grace it, is a palace.

LADY GIOVANNA.

In cottage or in palace, being still

Beyond your fortunes, you are still the king

Of courtesy and liberality.

COUNT.

I trust I still maintain my courtesy;

My liberality perforce is dead

Thro' lack of means of giving.

LADY GIOVANNA.

Yet I come

To ask a gift. [*Moves toward him a little.*

COUNT.

It will be hard, I fear,

To find one shock upon the field when all

The harvest has been carried.

LADY GIOVANNA.

But my boy—

(*Aside.*) No, no ! not yet—I cannot !

COUNT.

Ay, how is he,

That bright inheritor of your eyes—your boy ?

LADY GIOVANNA.

Alas, my Lord Federigo, he hath fallen

Into a sickness, and it troubles me.

COUNT.

Sick! is it so? why, when he came last year

To see me hawking, he was well enough:

And then I taught him all our hawking-phrases.

LADY GIOVANNA.

Oh yes, and once you let him fly your falcon.

COUNT.

How charm'd he was! what wonder?—A gallant boy,

A noble bird, each perfect of the breed.

LADY GIOVANNA (*sinks in chair*).

What do you rate her at?

COUNT.
                    My bird? a hundred

Gold pieces once were offer'd by the Duke.

I had no heart to part with her for money.

LADY GIOVANNA.

No, not for money. [COUNT *turns away and sighs.*

Wherefore do you sigh?

COUNT.

I have lost a friend of late.

LADY GIOVANNA.

I could sigh with you

For fear of losing more than friend, a son;

And if he leave me—all the rest of life—

That wither'd wreath were of more worth to me.

[*Looking at wreath on wall.*

COUNT.

That wither'd wreath is of more worth to me

Than all the blossom, all the leaf of this

New-wakening year. [*Goes and takes down wreath.*

LADY GIOVANNA.

And yet I never saw

The land so rich in blossom as this year.

COUNT (*holding wreath toward her*).

Was not the year when this was gather'd richer?

LADY GIOVANNA.

How long ago was that?

COUNT.

Alas, ten summers!

A lady that was beautiful as day

Sat by me at a rustic festival

With other beauties on a mountain meadow,

And she was the most beautiful of all;

Then but fifteen, and still as beautiful.

The mountain flowers grew thickly round about.

I made a wreath with some of these ; I ask'd

A ribbon from her hair to bind it with ;

I whisper'd, Let me crown you Queen of Beauty,

And softly placed the chaplet on her head.

A colour, which has colour'd all my life,

Flush'd in her face ; then I was call'd away ;

And presently all rose, and so departed.

Ah ! she had thrown my chaplet on the grass,

And there I found it.

> [*Lets his hands fall, holding wreath despondingly.*

LADY GIOVANNA (*after pause*).

> How long since do you say?

COUNT.

That was the very year before you married.

LADY GIOVANNA.

When I was married you were at the wars.

COUNT.

Had she not thrown my chaplet on the grass,

It may be I had never seen the wars.

[*Replaces wreath whence he had taken it.*

LADY GIOVANNA.

Ah, but, my lord, there ran a rumour then

That you were kill'd in battle.   I can tell you

True tears that year were shed for you in Florence.

COUNT.

It might have been as well for me.   Unhappily

I was but wounded by the enemy there

And then imprison'd.

LADY GIOVANNA.

Happily, however,

I see you quite recover'd of your wound.

COUNT.

No, no, not quite, Madonna, not yet, not yet.

Re-enter FILIPPO.

FILIPPO.

My lord, a word with you.

COUNT.

Pray, pardon me !

[LADY GIOVANNA *crosses, and passes behind chair
and takes down wreath ; then goes to chair by
table.*

COUNT (*to* FILIPPO).

What is it, Filippo ?

I

FILIPPO.

Spoons, your lordship.

COUNT.

Spoons !

FILIPPO.

Yes, my lord, for wasn't my lady born with a golden spoon in her ladyship's mouth, and we haven't never so much as a silver one for the golden lips of her ladyship.

COUNT.

Have we not half a score of silver spoons ?

FILIPPO.

Half o' one, my lord !

COUNT.

How half of one ?

FILIPPO.

I trod upon him even now, my lord, in my hurry, and broke him.

COUNT.

And the other nine?

FILIPPO.

Sold! but shall I not mount with your lordship's
leave to her ladyship's castle, in your lordship's and
her ladyship's name, and confer with her ladyship's
seneschal, and so descend again with some of her
ladyship's own appurtenances?

COUNT.

Why—no, man. Only see your cloth be clean.

[*Exit* FILIPPO.

LADY GIOVANNA.

Ay, ay, this faded ribbon was the mode
In Florence ten years back. What's here? a scroll
Pinn'd to the wreath.

My lord, you have said so much

Of this poor wreath that I was bold enough

To take it down, if but to guess what flowers

Had made it; and I find a written scroll

That seems to run in rhymings.   Might I read?

COUNT.

Ay, if you will.

LADY GIOVANNA.

It should be if you can.

(*Reads.*) "Dead mountain."   Nay, for who could

  trace a hand

So wild and staggering?

COUNT.

    This was penn'd, Madonna,

Close to the grating on a winter morn

In the perpetual twilight of a prison,

When he that made it, having his right hand

Lamed in the battle, wrote it with his left.

LADY GIOVANNA.

Oh heavens! the very letters seem to shake

With cold, with pain perhaps, poor prisoner! Well,

Tell me the words—or better—for I see

There goes a musical score along with them,

Repeat them to their music.

COUNT.

You can touch

No chord in me that would not answer you

In music.

LADY GIOVANNA.

That is musically said.

[COUNT *takes guitar.* LADY GIOVANNA *sits listen-*
ing with wreath in her hand, and quietly re-
moves scroll and places it on table at the end of
the song.

Count (*sings, playing guitar*).

"Dead mountain flowers, dead mountain-meadow

　flowers,

Dearer than when you made your mountain gay,

Sweeter than any violet of to-day,

Richer than all the wide world-wealth of May,

To me, tho' all your bloom has died away,

You bloom again, dead mountain-meadow flowers."

Enter Elisabetta *with cloth.*

Elisabetta.

A word with you, my lord !

Count (*singing*).

　　　　"O mountain flowers !"

Elisabetta.

A word, my lord ! (*Louder*).

Count (*sings*).

" Dead flowers ! "

Elisabetta.

A word, my lord !   (*Louder*).

Count.

I pray you pardon me again !

[Lady Giovanna, *looking at wreath.*

Count (*to* Elisabetta.)

What is it ?

Elisabetta.

My lord, we have but one piece of earthenware
to serve the salad in to my lady, and that cracked!

Count.

Why then, that flower'd bowl my ancestor
Fetch'd from the farthest east—we never use it

For fear of breakage—but this day has brought

A great occasion.   You can take it, nurse !

ELISABETTA.

I did take it, my lord, but what with my lady's

coming that had so flurried me, and what with the

fear of breaking it, I did break it, my lord: it is

broken !

COUNT.

My one thing left of value in the world !

No matter ! see your cloth be white as snow !

ELISABETTA (*pointing thro' window*).

White ?   I warrant thee, my son, as the snow yonder

on the very tip-top o' the mountain.

COUNT.

And yet to speak white truth, my good old mother,

I have seen it like the snow on the moraine.

ELISABETTA.

How can your lordship say so?   There, my lord!

[*Lays cloth.*

O my dear son, be not unkind to me.

And one word more.   [*Going—returns.*

COUNT (*touching guitar*).

Good! let it be but one.

ELISABETTA.

Hath she return'd thy love?

COUNT.

Not yet!

ELISABETTA.

And will she?

COUNT (*looking at* LADY GIOVANNA).

I scarce believe it!

ELISABETTA.

Shame upon her then ! [*Exit.*

COUNT (*sings.*)

" Dead mountain flowers "——

Ah well, my nurse has broken

The thread of my dead flowers, as she has broken

My china bowl.   My memory is as dead.

[*Goes and replaces guitar.*

Strange that the words at home with me so long

Should fly like bosom friends when needed most.

So by your leave if you would hear the rest,

The writing.

LADY GIOVANNA (*holding wreath toward him*).

There ! my lord, you are a poet,

And can you not imagine that the wreath,

Set, as you say, so lightly on her head,

Fell with her motion as she rose, and she,

A girl, a child, then but fifteen, however

Flutter'd or flatter'd by your notice of her,

Was yet too bashful to return for it?

COUNT.

Was it so indeed? was it so? was it so?

[*Leans forward to take wreath, and touches* LADY
GIOVANNA'S *hand, which she withdraws hastily;
he places wreath on corner of chair.*

LADY GIOVANNA (*with dignity*).

I did not say, my lord, that it was so;

I said you might imagine it was so.

Enter FILIPPO *with bowl of salad, which he places
on table.*

FILIPPO.

Here's a fine salad for my lady, for tho' we have

been a soldier, and ridden by his lordship's side, and
seen the red of the battle-field, yet are we now drill-
sergeant to his lordship's lettuces, and profess to be
great in green things and in garden-stuff.

LADY GIOVANNA.

I thank you, good Filippo.   [*Exit* FILIPPO.

Enter ELISABETTA *with bird on a dish which she
places on table.*

ELISABETTA (*close to table*).

Here's a fine fowl for my lady; I had scant time
to do him in.   I hope he be not underdone, for we
be undone in the doing of him.

LADY GIOVANNA.

I thank you, my good nurse.

FILIPPO (*re-entering with plate of prunes*).

And here are fine fruits for my lady—prunes, my lady, from the tree that my lord himself planted here in the blossom of his boyhood—and so I, Filippo, being, with your ladyship's pardon, and as your ladyship knows, his lordship's own foster-brother, would commend them to your ladyship's most peculiar appreciation.

[*Puts plate on table.*

ELISABETTA.

Filippo !

LADY GIOVANNA (COUNT *leads her to table*).

Will you not eat with me, my lord ?

COUNT.

I cannot,

Not a morsel, not one morsel. I have broken

My fast already. I will pledge you. Wine !

Filippo, wine !

[*Sits near table ;* FILIPPO *brings flask, fills the*
COUNT'S *goblet, then* LADY GIOVANNA'S ;
ELISABETTA *stands at the back of* LADY
GIOVANNA'S *chair.*

COUNT.

It is but thin and cold,

Not like the vintage blowing round your castle.

We lie too deep down in the shadow here.

Your ladyship lives higher in the sun.

[*They pledge each other and drink.*

LADY GIOVANNA.

If I might send you down a flask or two

Of that same vintage ?   There is iron in it.

It has been much commended as a medicine.

I give it my sick son, and if you be

Not quite recover'd of your wound, the wine

Might help you.   None has ever told me yet

The story of your battle and your wound.

FILIPPO (*coming forward*).

I can tell you, my lady, I can tell you.

ELISABETTA.

Filippo! will you take the word out of your master's

own mouth?

FILIPPO.

Was it there to take? Put it there, my lord.

COUNT.

Giovanna, my dear lady, in this same battle

We had been beaten—they were ten to one.

The trumpets of the fight had echo'd down,

I and Filippo here had done our best,

And, having passed unwounded from the field,

Were seated sadly at a fountain side,

Our horses grazing by us, when a troop,

Laden with booty and with a flag of ours

Ta'en in the fight——

FILIPPO.

Ay, but we fought for it back,

And kill'd——

ELISABETTA.

Filippo !

COUNT.

A troop of horse——

FILIPPO.

Five hundred !

COUNT.

Say fifty !

FILIPPO.

And we kill'd 'em by the score !

ELISABETTA.

Filippo !

FILIPPO.

Well, well, well !   I bite my tongue.

COUNT.

We may have left their fifty less by five.

However, staying not to count how many,

But anger'd at their flaunting of our flag,

We mounted, and we dashed into the heart of 'em.

I wore the lady's chaplet round my neck ;

It served me for a blessed rosary.

I am sure that more than one brave fellow owed

His death to the charm in it.

ELISABETTA.

Hear that, my lady !

COUNT.

I cannot tell how long we strove before

Our horses fell beneath us; down we went

Crush'd, hack'd at, trampled underfoot. The night,

As some cold-manner'd friend may strangely do us

K

The truest service, had a touch of frost

That help'd to check the flowing of the blood.

My last sight ere I swoon'd was one sweet face

Crown'd with the wreath.   *That* seem'd to come

  and go.

They left us there for dead !

ELISABETTA.

     Hear that, my lady !

FILIPPO.

Ay, and I left two fingers there for dead.   See,

my lady ! (*Showing his hand*).

LADY GIOVANNA.

I see, Filippo !

FILIPPO.

And I have small hope of the gentleman gout in

my great toe.

LADY GIOVANNA.

And why, Filippo?   [*Smiling absently.*

FILIPPO.

I left him there for dead too!

ELISABETTA.

She smiles at him—how hard the woman is!

My lady, if your ladyship were not

Too proud to look upon the garland, you

Would find it stain'd——

COUNT (*rising*).

Silence, Elisabetta!

ELISABETTA.

Stain'd with the blood of the best heart that ever

Beat for one woman.   [*Points to wreath on chair.*

LADY GIOVANNA (*rising slowly*).

I can eat no more!

COUNT.

You have but trifled with our homely salad,

But dallied with a single lettuce-leaf;

Not eaten anything.

LADY GIOVANNA.

　　　　　　Nay, nay, I cannot.

You know, my lord, I told you I was troubled.

My one child Florio lying still so sick,

I bound myself, and by a solemn vow,

That I would touch no flesh till he were well

Here, or else well in Heaven, where all is well.

[ELISABETTA *clears table of bird and salad:*
　　FILIPPO *snatches up the plate of prunes and*
　　holds them to LADY GIOVANNA.

FILIPPO.

But the prunes, my lady, from the tree that his

lordship——

LADY GIOVANNA.

Not now, Filippo.   My lord Federigo,

Can I not speak with you once more alone ?

COUNT.

You hear, Filippo ?   My good fellow, go !

FILIPPO.

But the prunes that your lordship——

ELISABETTA.

Filippo !

COUNT.

Ay, prune our company of thine own and go !

ELISABETTA.

Filippo !

FILIPPO (*turning*).

Well, well ! the women !   [*Exit.*

COUNT.

And thou too leave us, my dear nurse, alone.

ELISABETTA (*folding up cloth and going*).

And me too! Ay, the dear nurse will leave you

alone; but, for all that, she that has eaten the yolk

is scarce like to swallow the shell.

[*Turns and curtseys stiffly to* LADY GIOVANNA,
then exit. LADY GIOVANNA *takes out diamond
necklace from casket.*

LADY GIOVANNA.

I have anger'd your good nurse; these old-world
    servants

Are all but flesh and blood with those they serve.

My lord, I have a present to return you,

And afterwards a boon to crave of you.

COUNT.

No, my most honour'd and long-worshipt lady,

Poor Federigo degli Alberighi

Takes nothing in return from you except

Return of his affection—can deny

Nothing to you that you require of him.

LADY GIOVANNA.

Then I require you to take back your diamonds—

[*Offering necklace.*

I doubt not they are yours.   No other heart

Of such magnificence in courtesy

Beats—out of heaven.   They seem'd too rich a

prize

To trust with any messenger.   I came

In person to return them.   [*Count draws back.*

If the phrase

"Return" displease you, we will say—exchange them

For your—for your——

COUNT (*takes a step toward her and then back*).

     For mine—and what of mine?

LADY GIOVANNA.

Well, shall we say this wreath and your sweet

  rhymes?

COUNT.

But have you ever worn my diamonds?

LADY GIOVANNA.

         No!

For that would seem accepting of your love.

I cannot brave my brother—but be sure

That I shall never marry again, my lord!

COUNT.

Sure?

LADY GIOVANNA.

Yes !

COUNT.

Is this your brother's order ?

LADY GIOVANNA.

No !

For he would marry me to the richest man

In Florence; but I think you know the saying—

" Better a man without riches, than riches without a

man."

COUNT.

A noble saying—and acted on well would yield

A nobler breed of men and women.   Lady,

I find you a shrewd bargainer.   The wreath

That once you wore outvalues twentyfold

The diamonds that you never deign'd to wear.

But lay them there for a moment !

[*Points to table.*   LADY GIOVANNA *places*
necklace on table.*

And be you

Gracious enough to let me know the boon

By granting which, if aught be mine to grant,

I should be made more happy than I hoped

Ever to be again.

LADY GIOVANNA.

Then keep your wreath,

But you will find me a shrewd bargainer still.

I cannot keep your diamonds, for the gift

I ask for, to *my* mind and at this present

Outvalues all the jewels upon earth.

COUNT.

It should be love that thus outvalues all.

You speak like love, and yet you love me not.

I have nothing in this world but love for you.

LADY GIOVANNA.

Love? it *is* love, love for my dying boy,

Moves me to ask it of you.

COUNT.

What? my time?

Is it my time?   Well, I can give my time

To him that is a part of you, your son.

Shall I return to the castle with you?   Shall I

Sit by him, read to him, tell him my tales,

Sing him my songs?   You know that I can touch

The ghittern to some purpose.

LADY GIOVANNA.

No, not that!

I thank you heartily for that—and you,

I doubt not from your nobleness of nature,

Will pardon me for asking what I ask.

COUNT.

Giovanna, dear Giovanna, I that once

The wildest of the random youth of Florence

Before I saw you—all my nobleness

Of nature, as you deign to call it, draws

From you, and from my constancy to you.

No more, but speak.

LADY GIOVANNA.

        I will.   You know sick people,

More specially sick children, have strange fancies,

Strange longings; and to thwart them in their mood

May work them grievous harm at times, may even

Hasten their end.   I would you had a son !

It might be easier then for you to make

Allowance for a mother—her—who comes

To rob you of your one delight on earth.

How often has my sick boy yearn'd for this !

I have put him off as often ; but to-day

I dared not—so much weaker, so much worse

For last day's journey.   I was weeping for him ;

He gave me his hand : " I should be well again

If the good Count would give me——"

COUNT.

Give me.

LADY GIOVANNA.

His falcon.

COUNT (*starts back*).

My falcon !

LADY GIOVANNA.

Yes, your falcon, Federigo !

COUNT.

Alas, I cannot !

LADY GIOVANNA.

Cannot? Even so!

I fear'd as much.   O this unhappy world!

How shall I break it to him? how shall I tell him?

The boy may die: more blessed were the rags

Of some pale beggar-woman seeking alms

For her sick son, if he were like to live,

Than all my childless wealth, if mine must die.

I was to blame—the love you said you bore me—

My lord, we thank you for your entertainment,

> [*With a stately curtsey.*

And so return—Heaven help him!—to our son.

> [*Turns.*

COUNT (*rushes forward*).

Stay, stay, I am most unlucky, most unhappy.

You never had look'd in on me before,

And when you came and dipt your sovereign head

Thro' these low doors, you ask'd to eat with me.

I had but emptiness to set before you,

No not a draught of milk, no not an egg,

Nothing but my brave bird, my noble falcon,

My comrade of the house, and of the field.

She had to die for it—she died for you.

Perhaps I thought with those of old, the nobler

The victim was, the more acceptable

Might be the sacrifice. I fear you scarce

Will thank me for your entertainment now.

LADY GIOVANNA (*returning*).

I bear with him no longer.

COUNT.

No, Madonna!

And he will have to bear with it as he may.

LADY GIOVANNA.

I break with him for ever!

COUNT.

Yes, Giovanna,

But he will keep his love to you for ever!

LADY GIOVANNA.

You? you? not you! My brother! my hard
   brother!

O Federigo, Federigo, I love you!

Spite of ten thousand brothers, Federigo.

[*Falls at his feet.*

COUNT (*impetuously*).

Why then the dying of my noble bird

Hath served me better than her living—then

[*Takes diamonds from table*

These diamonds are both yours and mine—have won

Their value again—beyond all markets—there

I lay them for the first time round your neck.

> [*Lays necklace round her neck.*

And then this chaplet—No more feuds, but peace,

Peace and conciliation! I will make

Your brother love me. See, I tear away

The leaves were darken'd by the battle—

> [*Pulls leaves off and throws them down.*

> —crown you

Again with the same crown my Queen of Beauty.

> [*Places wreath on her head.*

Rise—I could almost think that the dead garland

Will break once more into the living blossom.

Nay, nay, I pray you rise.

> [*Raises her with both hands.*

> We two together

Will help to heal your son—your son and mine—

L

We shall do it—we shall do it.   [*Embraces her.*

The purpose of my being is accomplish'd,

And I am happy !

LADY GIOVANNA.

And I too, Federigo.

THE END.

Printed by R. & R. CLARK, *Edinburgh.*

Crown 8vo.   Price 7s. 6d.

THE WORKS OF

LORD TENNYSON

POET LAUREATE.

A NEW COLLECTED EDITION.

CORRECTED THROUGHOUT BY THE AUTHOR.

With a New Portrait.

———

MACMILLAN AND CO., LONDON.

LORD TENNYSON'S WORKS.

THE ORIGINAL EDITIONS.
Fcap. 8vo.

	S.	D.
POEMS	6	0
MAUD, AND OTHER POEMS . . .	3	6
THE PRINCESS	3	6
IDYLLS OF THE KING (COLLECTED) . .	6	0
ENOCH ARDEN, ETC.	3	6
THE HOLY GRAIL, AND OTHER POEMS	4	6
IN MEMORIAM	4	0
BALLADS, AND OTHER POEMS . .	5	0
HAROLD: A DRAMA.	6	0
QUEEN MARY: A DRAMA . . .	6	0
THE LOVER'S TALE	3	6

MACMILLAN AND CO., LONDON.